Hedgehog and Rabbit

The Stubborn Cloud
Hedgehog and Rabbit Collection

© Text: Pablo Albo, 2016
© Illustrations: Gómez, 2016
© Edition: NubeOcho, 2017
www.nubeocho.com – info@nubeocho.com

Original title: *La nube cabezota*
Translator: Kim Griffin
Text editing: Ben Dawlatly and Rebecca Packard

Distributed in the United States by
Consortium Book Sales & Distribution

First edition: 2017
ISBN: 978-84-945971-9-0

Printed in China by Asia Pacific Offset,
respecting international labor standards.

Hedgehog and Rabbit

The Stubborn Cloud

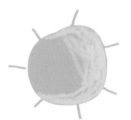

PABLO ALBO
ILLUSTRATED BY
GÓMEZ

nubeOCHO

Hedgehog and Rabbit
were in the garden.
Rabbit was eating cabbages.
Hedgehog was looking for snails.

A cow was eating grass
out in the field.

And off in the distance,
a crow pecked at
a cauliflower.

It was a sunny day.

All of sudden, the sun went away, and it became very dark. Rabbit got very scared and hid in a hollow tree trunk.

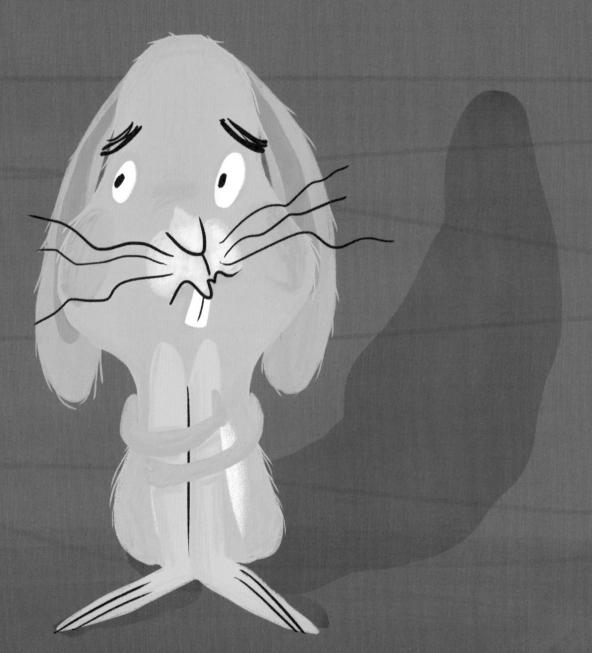

Hedgehog looked up at the sky and saw that a cloud had covered the sun.

One single cloud in the middle of the sky.

"Hey, Cloud!" said Hedgehog. "Please move aside a little, you are blocking the sun!"

But the cloud wouldn't move.

Rabbit came out of
his hiding place and
said to the cloud,

"Hey, Cloud! Move aside! There is lots of
room in the sky!"

But the cloud wouldn't move then either.

Then Rabbit said to Hedgehog,

"I think the problem is that she is too far away to hear us."
"Well, then let's climb up the tree," suggested Hedgehog.
"Good idea!" said Rabbit.

Rabbit jumped up onto the lowest branch and waited for Hedgehog. But he was taking too long.

"Hedgehog, aren't you coming up?"
"Oh... yes, Rabbit, I just got a little distracted because this trunk is full of snails. I'll be right up."

And so the two of them, from way up high in the fig tree, yelled to the cloud:

"Hey, Cloud! Move aside a little. You are blocking the sun!"

But the cloud paid no attention to them.

"We are still too far away for her to hear us," said Hedgehog.

"Well, then let's climb higher up," suggested Rabbit.

And in two short hops, Rabbit jumped to the highest part of the fig tree and waited for Hedgehog. When he saw that Hedgehog was taking a long time, he looked down and shouted,

"Hey, Hedgehog! Leave those snails alone and come up here!"

"No, Rabbit, that's not the problem. I am a hedgehog, so it's not as easy for me to jump up there as it is for you. Why don't you talk to the cloud?"

"All right," said Rabbit.

"Cloud, listen, we are cold. Would you be so kind as to move aside?"

But the cloud paid no attention.

"Maybe she just can't hear me," said Rabbit.
"That just can't be. I heard you perfectly,"
said Hedgehog.
"But you are closer to me than she is,"
explained Rabbit.

"Yes, that is true. Can you see
anyone who could help us?"
"There is a crow pecking at the
cauliflowers."

"Crow, you can fly. Could you please fly up close to the cloud and tell her to move aside?" said Rabbit.

But the crow didn't hear him either.

"Did he do what you asked him to do, Rabbit?"

"No."

"Maybe the crow is too far away," said Hedgehog.

"No, it is the cloud that is far away; the crow is closer," said Rabbit.

"Maybe the crow is far away and the cloud is even farther away," answered Hedgehog.

"Yes, maybe that's it."

"Rabbit, do you see anyone closer than the crow?"
"Yes, there is a cow eating grass out in the field,"
answered Rabbit.
"Well, ask her to help us," suggested Hedgehog.
"But cows can't fly!" said Rabbit.

"I know, but you can ask the cow to ask the crow to fly up and talk to the cloud."

"What a great idea!"

"Cow, please ask the crow to talk to the cloud," said Rabbit.

The cow didn't hear him either. And even though she might have heard Rabbit, she wouldn't have understood him, because cows don't speak the same language as rabbits or crows.

Just then, the cow
happened to moo.

The loud moo
frightened the crow,
and he flew away.

He flew right over the fig tree and went higher in the sky, near the cloud, looking for another garden where he could peck in peace with no cows nearby to frighten him.

Just then, the wind blew the cloud aside.

The sun shone again, and Rabbit and Hedgehog felt its warm rays.

"Thank you, Cow," said Rabbit.
"Thank you, Cloud," said Hedgehog.

"Thank you, Fig Tree," said Rabbit.
"Thank you, Crow," said Hedgehog.

"Hello, Sun!" said both of them together.